Seven Magic Brothers

七兄弟

English / Chinese

Retold by **Kuang-Tsai Hao**   *Illustrated by* **Eva Wang**
English translation by **Rick Charette**

遠流出版公司
YUAN-LIOU PUBLISHING CO., LTD.

Long ago, there was an old, good-hearted couple, who lived all by themselves. One morning, while the wife washed clothes by the river, a cloud of smoke arose. A great spirit appeared. He said, "Here are seven golden pills. Eat one each day, and soon you'll finally have children."

But the wife could not wait. She ate all seven. Her stomach grew bigger and bigger each day. In autumn she gave birth to seven bouncing baby boys!

從前，有一對老夫妻心腸非常好，結婚三十年連一個孩子也沒有。有天，太太到河邊洗衣裳，忽然，水面升起一陣煙，出現一個神仙。神仙說：「這裡有七顆金丹，一天吃一顆，就能生娃娃。」

她拿了七顆金丹，一口氣全吞下，肚子一天比一天大，終於生下七胞胎，全都是男孩。

The seven brothers grew quickly. Each was blessed with a special power; the eldest had great strength, the second had super hearing, the third was harder than iron, the fourth could bore through earth, the fifth was nonflammable, the sixth could stretch endlessly, and the

youngest could swallow anything.

　　一年年過去，七個兄弟都長大了，雖然他們的
面貌和聲音都一樣，但每個都有超能力。老大力
氣大，老二耳朵靈，老三硬鐵漢，老四能鑽土，
老五不怕火，老六踩高腳，老七張大口。

One day, taking a break from their heavy fieldwork, the brothers heard a bugle call. It was the Emperor on parade! The procession was an awesome sight, the long march of soldiers winding like a coiled dragon. Then, suddenly, a huge boulder came crashing down the mountainside...

一天中午，七兄弟忙完農事，正在田邊休息，皇帝出巡的隊伍正巧經過，那隊伍既浩大又威風，他們走呀走的，忽然從山上滾下一塊大石頭…

The boulder tumbled straight for the Emperor! But at the last second someone shot up and brought the boulder to a screeching halt. Who was the hero? Who else but the eldest brother! The Emperor offered him a high post, but he said no. He was offered treasure and gold, but still said no. The surprised Emperor could not but let him go home.

　　眼看大石頭就要砸中皇帝的馬車，這時一個人影閃出，及時把石頭接住，那人正是七兄弟中的老大。

　　老大救了皇帝一命，皇帝非常高興，一定要重賞他，但老大不肯做官，也不想發財，皇帝拿他沒辦法，只好讓他回家。

Returning to the Palace, the Emperor's heart was uneasy. "Such a small fellow, yet so strong. He has no love of wealth, so I have no control of him. He may be trouble one day." The Emperor could not sleep, until an evil plan was set... "That's it. I shall arrest him and have his head chopped off."

回宮後，皇帝越想越不對勁：「那個少年郎本領這麼強，萬一哪一天，他想要造反，可就麻煩了！不如找個藉口，抓他來砍頭。」

Second brother had powerful hearing, so heard the evil plan. The next day, third brother was seized and taken by the Emperor's men.

老二耳朵靈，皇帝的話順著風，傳進他耳中。第二天大隊兵馬把老三捉去。

Third brother was dragged into the palace. The
Emperor ordered his head axed off. But third brother
was harder than iron, so nothing could harm him.
Dozens of swords were broken, but only three hairs
were cut from his head. The Emperor was furious,
and ordered him burned alive first thing next morning.

老三被抓到皇宮，皇帝立刻命令刀斧手
砍下老三的腦袋，哪知老三硬鐵漢，不怕
大刀砍。刀斧手砍得手發麻，只砍斷三根
頭髮，皇帝越看越氣，下令明天一早，用
火燒死他。

Late that night, fourth brother secretly bore past the walls of the fortified city, with the fifth following close behind. They drilled under the prison walls, up to where third brother had been locked up. Fifth brother took third's place. No need to worry now; just to wait for the show to begin!

老四能鑽土，他帶著老五，偷偷的在挖地道。他們挖過城牆，終於找到關著老三的牢房。老五立刻爬進去，把老三給換出來，看來明天有好戲上場了。

At dawn soldiers escorted fifth brother to a tall scaffold with stacked firewood underneath. Fifth brother was tightly tied on top.

第二天天亮，士兵把老五綁在刑場的高台上，準備放火燒死他。

The fire was set and soon
blazed high. But fifth brother
was nonflammable. Fiery red
flames licked the sky, yet he
just smiled! He was taken to
his cell once again.

老五不怕火,再大的火也傷不了他。皇帝只好又將他
關進大牢。

Fifth brother pretended to talk in his sleep. "I cannot be chopped, nor burned. My only fear is falling to my death." The guards reported to the Emperor. Fifth brother was at once brought to a high cliff, and shoved toward the edge...

老五在牢房，假裝說夢話：「我天不怕地不怕，就怕摔。還好沒有人知道。」牢房守衛一聽，馬上跑去向皇帝報告。

皇帝叫人把老五帶到山崖邊，想要摔死他。

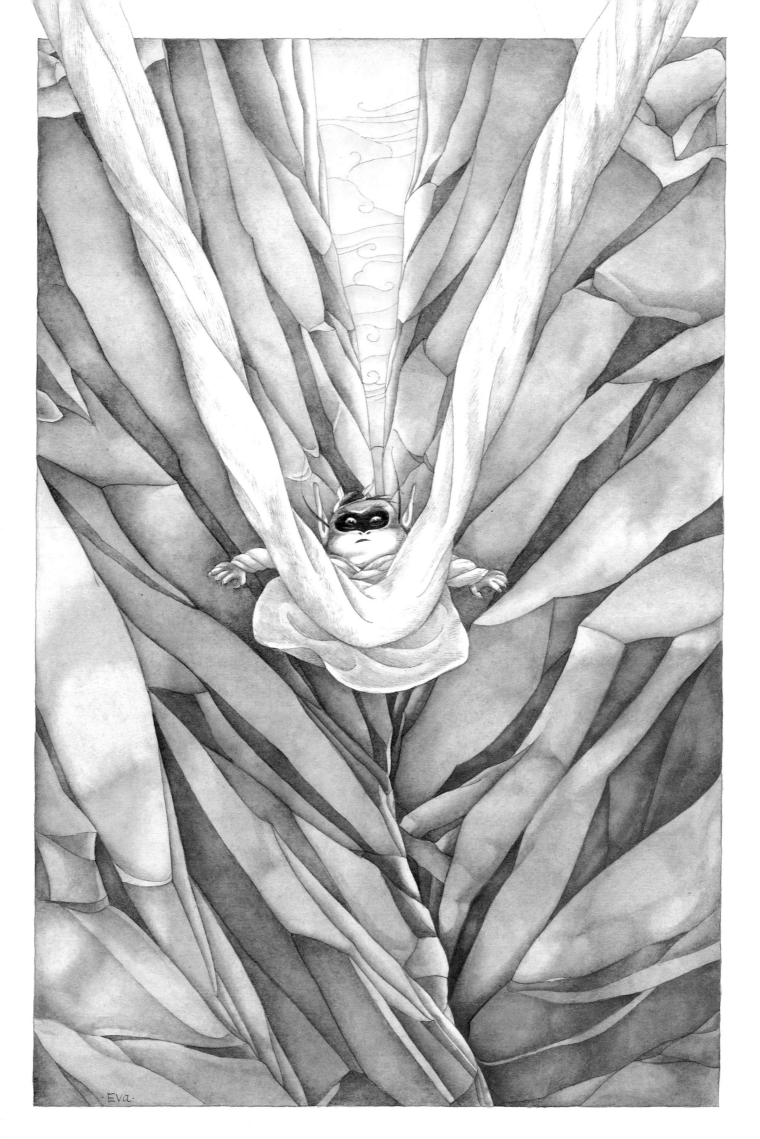

But it wasn't fifth brother that was pushed over —— it was sixth! Sixth brother's legs stretched and stretched, until his feet softly reached the bottom. His body was now higher than the cliffsides! He then hopped back out and ran home. The troops madly dashed after him.

老六踩高腳，雙腳一伸長，人比山還高。原來被推下去的不是老五，是老六。老六拔腿就跑，皇帝氣極了，帶著軍隊拚命追。

In wild and hot pursuit, the Emperor was suddenly blocked by seventh brother, who said, "As long as you do not throw me into the sea, I promise to obey you." Of course, he was at once knocked down, tied up, taken out to sea, and tossed -- Sploosh! -- over the side.

皇帝追到半路，被老七擋住。「只要不把我丟進大海中，我就乖乖聽話…」老七話還沒說完，就被綁上船。皇帝親自領兵出海，噗通一聲，老七被丟進海中。

Soon, the surface became quiet and calm. Not a ripple. The Emperor broke into a big grin; he believed his enemy was now fish food.

Suddenly there was a thunderous BOOM. The ship's bottom crunched down on the rocky ocean floor. Where was all the water? Seventh brother had sucked the ocean completely dry!

海面風平浪靜，見不到一絲波動。皇帝心裡正高興，他想老七這下準沒命。忽然轟隆一聲，船底被卡在石頭上！原來是張大口老七，一口氣就把海水喝光光。

He strolled back to the shore, then turned around with mouth spread wide. The water exploded back out like a gigantic sea dragon, shaking the earth.

老七走回岸邊，一轉身就張大口，海水就像一條巨龍般衝口而出。

Monstrous waves rushed and roared, one second
swallowing up the ship, the next spitting it sky-high.
A few moments later the ship disappeared. Where did
the Emperor and his ship go? Nobody knows.

巨波大浪向前衝，一下把船吞入海中，一下把船抬上半空。沒
幾下，船就不見了，只留下海浪滔滔。皇帝和船被沖到哪裡去了
？沒有人知道。

The sun began to shine like
gold, and its rays danced over the sea.
Now the seven magic brothers gathered together
again, shoulder to shoulder. They were all of one
heart, with no other wish but to live in peace and
enjoy the cool ocean breeze.

太陽把金黃色的光，投在海面上。七個兄弟，一種心情，
只想靜靜的看著陽光，享受涼涼的海風。

Seven Magic Brothers

English／Chinese

Retold by Kuang-Tsai Hao; Illustrated by Eva Wang

English translation by Rick Charette

Copyright © 1994 by Yuan-Liou Publishing Co., Ltd.

All rights reserved.

7F-5, No. 184, Sec. 3, Ding Chou Rd., Taipei, Taiwan, R.O.C.

TEL: (886-2) 3651212   FAX: (886-2) 3657979

Printed in Taiwan